04-296
W9-CDG-807

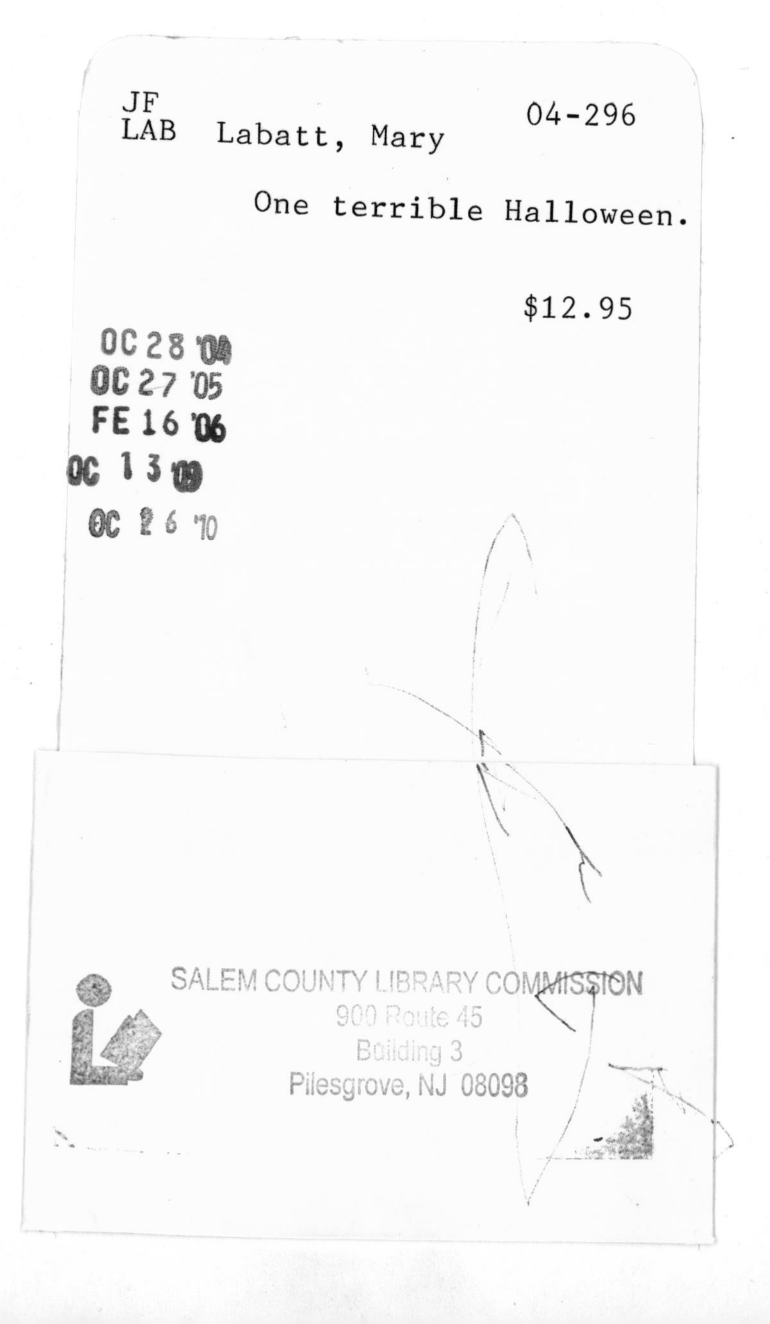
JF
LAB Labatt, Mary
04-296
One terrible Halloween.
$12.95
OC 28 '04
OC 27 '05
FE 16 '06
OC 13 '09
OC 26 '10
SALEM COUNTY LIBRARY COMMISSION
900 Route 45
Building 3
Pilesgrove, NJ 08098

ONE TERRIBLE HALLOWEEN

MARY LABATT

KIDS CAN PRESS

Kids Can Press acknowledges the financial support of the Ontario Arts Council, the Canada Council for the Arts and the Government of Canada, through the BPIDP, for our publishing activity.

Published in Canada by
Kids Can Press Ltd.
29 Birch Avenue
Toronto, ON M4V 1E2

Published in the U.S. by
Kids Can Press Ltd.
2250 Military Road
Tonawanda, NY 14150

www.kidscanpress.com

Edited by Charis Wahl
Designed by Marie Bartholomew
Typeset by Sherill Chapman
Printed and bound in Canada

CM 02 0 9 8 7 6 5 4 3 2 1
CM PA 02 0 9 8 7 6 5 4 3 2 1

National Library of Canada Cataloguing in Publication Data

Labatt, Mary, date.
One terrible Halloween

ISBN 1-55337-138-0 (bound) ISBN 1-55337-139-9 (pbk.)

1. Halloween — Juvenile fiction. I. Title. II. Series: Labatt, Mary, date.
Sam, dog detective.

PS8573.A135O54 2002 jC813'.54 C2001-902943-8
PZ7.L114On 2002

Kids Can Press is a Corus™ Entertainment company

To Rick and Jane and their families —
with my love

1. Halloween is Coming

Squinting through the window, Sam watched dry leaves swirling over the lawn and the dark street. A ghostly wind rattled the bare branches.

Looks like a good night for a mystery. Sam glared around at the empty living room and sighed. *Hmph. I'm a famous detective and I'm locked in here with no case*. In disgust, she hopped off the couch and went to the kitchen to nose around for a snack.

Joan and Bob should come home, Sam growled to herself as she sniffed at the kitchen floor. *It's bad enough when they work all day. They have no business leaving me alone at night*.

She eyed the phone on the wall. *Too bad I*

can't use that thing. I could call Jennie. She'd bring me some food.

Sitting on the kitchen floor with a thud, Sam tried to send her thoughts to Jennie. *Get over here, Jennie. I'm bored, and I'm starving.*

Ten-year-old Jennie Levinsky was Sam's next-door neighbor and her best friend. Joan and Bob had hired Jennie to take Sam for walks when they were at work. So Jennie came every day after school.

When Sam first met Jennie, she knew she'd found someone who could hear her. *I always know when someone has the gift,* Sam told her new friend. *Most dogs are too stupid to notice.*

Jennie was amazed. Sam's thoughts rang in her head like an echo. No one else could hear Sam, not even Jennie's best friend, Beth Morrison. And it was a secret. No one knew about it except the three of them.

Sam squeezed her eyes shut and thought hard. *Hey, Jennie! Ask if you can come over here. I'm all alone. Bring me some watermelon … and a banana and jam sandwich … and some nachos with butterscotch sauce ... I'm hungry!*

Sam waited. But nothing happened.

Phooey. The kid's deaf.

In the house next door, Jennie was in her bedroom doing homework when she felt Sam's call. She stopped writing.

"Sam's hungry," she giggled. She shrugged. "Sam's always hungry."

Then Jennie heard the echo again. Sam was telling her to come right over. Putting down her pencil, Jennie went to ask her mother if she could get Sam.

Mrs. Levinsky raised her eyebrows. "At this time of night?"

"Joan and Bob have gone out. I think she's lonely."

Jennie's mother smiled. "Go and get her then. She can stay until nine o'clock."

Noel, Jennie's thirteen-year-old brother,

lifted his spiky blond head from his computer game. "Did that walking mop tell you she's lonely?" he smirked.

Jennie ignored him. "Thanks, Mom." She let herself out the front door and ran across the lawn to Sam's house.

Sam heard the key. At the front door, she leaped on Jennie and slobbered and whined and licked. She poked her nose in Jennie's pockets. *So, where's the snack I ordered?*

Jennie's brown eyes twinkled. "At my house. My mom says you can come over."

Good. Sam marched to the door and stared. *What are we waiting for?*

Sam shoved through the door and dashed across the lawn to Jennie's house.

I need food, Jennie. And I need it bad.

Jennie smuggled a bowl of strawberry Jell-O and some bacon chips up to her room.

Yum. Sam stuck her nose in the bowl and slurped.

Jennie spread chips on the floor and watched while Sam chomped and crunched. Bits of chips spewed out of her mouth as she chewed.

When she finished, Sam belched and licked her whiskers. *Whew! Joan and Bob are trying to starve me. I keep telling you to call the Humane Society.*

Jennie giggled. "They just want you to eat dog food."

Sam's tufty eyebrows shot up. *Tell me you're kidding. Nobody would eat cat guts.*

"It's good for you, Sam. All dogs eat dog food."

Sam glared. *If you think it's so good, you —*

"I'm not having the dog food fight again, Sam." Jennie held up her hand. "We've been over this a thousand times."

Sam sniffed. *Don't mention dog food to me again — ever.*

Hopping up on Jennie's bed, Sam peered out the window. Whispering leaves rolled down the empty street. *Looks nice and spooky out there, doesn't it?*

Jennie glanced at the street and shrugged. "Looks like an ordinary fall night to me."

Ordinary is bad. Sam sighed. *I need excitement.*

She turned to Jennie, the hair over her eyes moving up and down. *I can't stand it. There's no ghost in my house. I haven't found any monsters around here. I can't even find any crooks.*

Sam slumped down on the bed. *I'm a detective, Jennie. I need a case.*

"Cheer up," Jennie giggled. "It's only a week until Halloween. We'll have loads of fun then."

Sudden shivers of happiness shot through Sam. She sat bolt upright. *I forgot about Halloween!*

She glanced outside at the dark clouds and the long black shadows creeping over the empty street. In her mind, she saw the sidewalk seething with monsters and vampires and witches. The moon was full, the night was dark and the air crackled with magic. Every terrible thing came out of its grave dragging its shredded grave clothes … looking for victims.

Halloween is wonderful! Anything can happen on Halloween!

Sam closed her eyes, her mind alive with horrible creatures from the dark regions of the earth …

I hope every ghost and goblin and monster in the world comes out this year …

The scarier the better.

2. The Three Witches of Woodford

After school the next day, Sam lolled on Jennie's pillows, nibbling chips off the bedspread. She scowled. *Where's the ketchup, Jennie? These things need some zip.*

But Jennie wasn't listening. She and Beth were talking about Halloween.

"I'd like to go as a princess," said Jennie dreamily. "Or a fairy."

Yuk. Sam snorted. *My friend, the wimp*.

"I am not a wimp." Jennie looked hurt. "I like fairies."

Sam snorted again. *Fairies are no good for Halloween. Halloween is for ghosts and monsters and vampires and weird things coming out of graves.*

"I feel so left out when you and Sam have your conversations!" exclaimed Beth, shaking her fluffy red hair. "Does Sam hate princesses and fairies?"

Jennie rolled her eyes. "Yeah. She thinks they're wimpy."

"But she likes Halloween, doesn't she?"

"Loves it. She wants to see monsters."

"Let's take Sam trick-or-treating this year." Beth grinned at the big dog.

Sam's head whipped up. *Good idea. I want the biggest treat bag in Woodford.*

"I think we should make her a costume." Beth's green eyes sparkled.

"I know!" Jennie clapped her hands. "Let's make her some huge ears. She can be a rabbit."

Sam groaned. *Forget rabbits. I want to be a monster ... or a terrible alien with a blood-sucking tongue.*

Jennie sighed. "Sam wants to be a monster — or a weird alien."

Beth crammed a handful of chips in her mouth. "Let's make a monster costume with warts all over it."

Hmmm ... I like warts ... Witches have warts.

Jennie snapped her fingers. "Sam could be a witch!"

Beth's face lit up. "We can all be witches!"

Witches are good.

"Three witches ..." Jennie thought for a moment. "Sounds good."

"That's it!" exclaimed Beth. "We'll be the three witches of Woodford."

We'll be horrible, creepy, hag witches. Little kids will scream when they see us. They'll run away and drop all their candy ...

I love Halloween.

That night, Sam lay on the floor while Joan and Bob watched television. A lady in a ghost costume was announcing something.

Sam looked up.

"Don't forget, folks," the ghost was saying.

"All this week it's Scary Movie Week."

Hmmm ... Scary is nice.

Sam watched as the ghost flew up to a haunted house. Bats came screeching out of the windows. The ghost hovered over the house. "Every night until Halloween, tune in at seven o'clock for the scariest movies ever!" Then she disappeared in a wisp of smoke.

Sam settled her chin on her paws.

I love scary movies.

Almost as much as I love Halloween.

3. Scary Movie Week

"Scary movie week is great!" cried Beth the next day. "Did you see the one last night? It was all about a creature of the deep?"

"I hate horror movies." Jennie shivered.

Sam glared. *And I hate wimps.*

Jennie shivered again. "Noel says tonight's movie is about an evil spirit who lives in the walls of an old house."

Sounds good.

"Great!" Beth's eyes sparkled. "I'm doing my homework now so I can watch it."

Just then Jennie's mother poked her head into the room. "I brought some black bristol board from the drugstore. It's perfect for making witch hats."

Sam eyed the shiny cardboard. *That stuff doesn't look very scary*.

"This is how you do it." Jennie's mother rolled a piece. "Make a cone and staple it. Then cut this bit off and I'll help you do the brim." She perched the long black cone on Jennie's head.

Phooey. Where's the good stuff? I want warty noses ... claws for fingernails ... cracked lips oozing pus ... stuff like that!

"You staple your hats while I make dinner," said Mrs. Levinsky.

When Jennie's mother was gone, Sam looked scornfully at the black bristol board. *Hats are boring. I want something horrible to wear, something terrifying.*

"Quit trying to scare everybody, Sam." Jennie started to roll her hat. "Halloween is spooky enough without you making it worse."

I've never made anything worse in my life. Sam sniffed. *I make things better*.

"We're going to have fun on Halloween,

Sam." Beth smiled lovingly at the big sheepdog as she made her hat.

Sam's pink tongue hung out of her mouth. *These hats are dumb. We need to meet some real witches on Halloween.*

"I don't want to meet witches." Jennie chewed her lip. "There won't be any real witches out on Halloween anyway."

That's what you think. Hope you don't wimp out.

Jennie gritted her teeth. "We won't meet any witches."

You're wrong, Jennie. We'll meet lots of weird things. There'll be goblins and monsters and vampires and mutants walking around. Sam shuddered happily. *I want to meet them all.*

"Quit scaring me, Sam." Jennie stapled her hat firmly. "Halloween's a fun time to dress up and get candy. It's not real."

Sam gasped. *Of course it's real. We might even meet Frankenstein.*

"This dog is crazy, Beth. She thinks real monsters come out on Halloween."

Watch who you call crazy. I might bite.

Beth thought for a moment. "Well … Maybe they do."

Sam shot Jennie a nasty look.

I love Beth.

4. The Story of the Ghouls

On the third night the scary movie was about ghouls. Shrieking, they came out of their graves. They roamed through the village looking for anyone who had harmed them when they were alive. The villagers screamed and hid in their houses. Sam shuddered with happiness.

The next day, Beth told Jennie and Sam about a book she got from the library. It was about the spookiest Halloween legends of all time.

Ask her if that book has ghouls in it. Sam stared at Jennie.

"Sam wants to know if there are any ghouls in the book."

"Well ... There was one story that scared

me a lot," admitted Beth.

Tell us.

"Don't tell us," said Jennie grimly. "Noel won't shut up about last night's movie. I don't want to hear any more scary stories."

Sam nudged Jennie with her big black nose. *Tell Beth we want the story.*

Jennie sighed. "Sam wants to hear the story, Beth."

Beth smiled as she dug in her school bag. "I brought the book to show you."

Beth flipped through the book and held up a picture of sinister creatures sneaking out of a dark wood. They wore black cloaks, and their faces were hidden by huge hoods. Thousands of them were streaming out of the forest.

Looks good. Sam settled on Jennie's pillows and gobbled three butter tarts. *What's the story?*

"These are ghouls — just like I saw in the movie," Beth went on. "Every hundred years they come out of the forest on Halloween night."

Sam's ears pricked up. *Sounds good.*

"Halloween night has to be dark and foggy,"

Beth went on. "They won't come if there's a moon."

Jennie hid her face in her hands. "They're horrible."

But Beth didn't stop. "Here's how the legend goes …"

Get to the good part.

Jennie clapped her hands over her ears, but Beth didn't notice.

"If Halloween night is dark and really foggy — and if it's been a hundred years …" Beth paused and grinned at Sam with sparkling eyes. "… the ghouls come out."

Love it.

Beth lowered her voice. "They creep through the town looking for children. At the stroke of midnight, they drag all the kids back into the forest."

Jennie gulped. "C-can the kids get away?"

Beth shook her head. "Nope." She turned a page. "When they get to the forest, they turn all the captured kids into ghouls!"

Jennie gasped.

"That's how they make new ghouls." Beth chewed on her thumbnail. "Every hundred years they grab new kids."

I wonder if they want dogs.

"One kid escaped — but only one."

"Who w-was it?" Jennie's eyes were wide.

Probably a famous, intelligent sheepdog. Sam licked at the side of the popcorn bag. *Hey, will somebody open this?*

Jennie leaned over and ripped open the bag.

Now, where's the ketchup?

"No ketchup, Sam," said Jennie firmly. "My mom was really mad about the spots on the bedspread last week."

She doesn't understand good food. Sam eyed the popcorn suspiciously. *How can anybody eat this without ketchup?*

Jennie ignored Sam. "Who escaped, Beth?"

"A boy about six years old," answered Beth. "When he saw the ghouls, he wasn't scared. He laughed at them!"

Sam looked up from the popcorn. *That's my kind of kid.*

"D-didn't the ghouls g-get mad?"

"That's the strange part. They let him go." Beth looked back at the picture. "Ghouls can't capture someone who isn't scared of them."

They won't take me then. I wouldn't be scared of some dumb-looking guys in black capes. What's so special about ghouls anyway?

"What are ghouls like?" asked Jennie.

"When they're not in the woods, they live in cemeteries and they only come out at night. And ..." Beth held the book close to her chest. "... they eat people."

Jennie shuddered.

Just as long as they don't eat dogs.

Beth turned a page and showed another picture. Enormous ghouls held screaming children under their arms as they fled through the night. Mothers and fathers were running out into the street crying and begging the ghouls to stop.

"D-doesn't anybody ever get their kids back?" asked Jennie in a small voice.

"Never." Beth shook her head. "Once a

ghoul's got you, you're toast."

Jennie eyed the picture. Held prisoner under one of the ghoul's arms, a girl was screaming. She had long brown hair and she looked about ten years old — just like Jennie. A sick feeling started in the pit of Jennie's stomach. She couldn't take her eyes off the picture.

At last, Beth turned the page. In the next picture ghouls were creeping through the forest, carrying the children toward a huge cave.

"This isn't true!" cried Jennie suddenly. "It's just a legend!"

"It might be true." Beth chewed a fingernail.

Of course, it's true. Anything that weird has to be true. Who ever heard of somebody living in a cemetery?

Sam's mind started to race. She pictured a cemetery at night, its tombstones gleaming in the moonlight. While ghosts circled overhead, black-cloaked ghouls crept between the stones. Sam shivered deliciously.

Wonderful.

I hope those guys come to Woodford.

5. The Year of the Ghouls

That night, Sam watched from the upstairs window as fog rolled over Woodford. Out of the fields it came. Gray, thick mist crept over houses and backyards until Sam couldn't see anything.

Downstairs, the music for Scary Movie Week was playing on TV, but Sam didn't go down to watch. She stayed at the window.

Fog, huh?

All evening, Sam kept going back to the window to check the fog. But it didn't lift. The night just got foggier and foggier.

At last Sam thumped down the stairs to the front door and whined.

"Do you want to go out, Sam?" Joan got up and opened the door.

Sam stepped outside, sat on the front porch and looked into the thick mist. *They say it has to be foggy when the ghouls come … Hmmm …*

She listened. Far, far away she could hear a hubbub of voices.

Sounds like the ghouls are getting ready in those woods over by the old airfield.

Sam listened again.

I bet this is the year they come.

I just know it.

"Stop scaring me!" yelled Jennie, as she dished raspberry ice cream into a bowl for Sam. "I don't want to think about ghouls!"

No need to yell. All I said was, this could be the year.

Beth poured ketchup on the ice cream and made a face. "This dog eats the craziest stuff."

Sam glared. *I hate it when you two insult me. I happen to be a very special dog.*

"We know you're special, Sam. But don't talk about scary stuff." Jennie opened a package of cookies and put six of them on the floor for Sam.

I have to talk about scary stuff. It's Halloween.

Jennie sighed.

Get a grip, Jennie. You're turning into a huge wimp.

Woodford was a sleepy little town nestled in rolling farmland. Usually, the houses looked peaceful and cozy. But when Jennie and Beth and Sam went for a walk that day, the town had changed.

Skeletons hung in windows. Jack-o'-lanterns leered from porches. One house had huge spiders crawling on the roof. Another had tombstones on the front lawn.

Sam danced up and down the streets. *Looks great, doesn't it?*

"Let's go home and try on our costumes," said Jennie suddenly. "My mom made the capes yesterday, and I finished our hats."

Sam stopped in her tracks. *Capes and hats aren't going to scare anybody. Get me a mask that'll make people scream.*

Jennie rolled her eyes. "Who ever heard of a dog in a mask?"

"Sam, you can hardly see now with all that hair over your eyes!" Beth grinned. "If we put a mask on you, you won't see anything." She hooted as she pictured Sam tripping over her loot bag.

Sam shot Beth a nasty look. *Sheepdogs are supposed to have hair over their eyes.*

Jennie looked lovingly at Sam's huffy face. "Admit it, Sam. A mask would make it really hard for you to see."

Oh, shut up.

When the three friends got back to Jennie's house, they noticed that daylight was fading quickly.

"Look at that!" cried Jennie, watching fog settle on her roof.

"Fog," said Beth in a strange voice.

Ha! Sam chortled to herself. *What did I tell you? When the ghouls come, it has to be very foggy.*

"I remember," said Jennie, her face suddenly pale. She looked up and down the street as mist crept over the housetops.

"It's thick, isn't it?" she said hollowly.

"Yeah." Beth watched as everything around them became dim and gray and shadowy.

You bet it's thick! Sam spun around. *I tell you, Jennie — this is it!*

"You don't suppose this is the year of the ghouls, do you, Beth?"

Beth gulped. "Sure looks like it."

Yahoo! Sam did a little dance in the driveway. *Excitement at last!*

6. Something Strange

When the three friends tried on their costumes, Sam worked herself into a fury. Jennie tied the witch hat onto Sam's head with a huge bow. Then she put a long back cape around Sam's shoulders.

Jennie stood back to admire the costume. "Sam makes a wonderful witch."

Sam glared at the mirror and growled. *I don't look like a witch. I look like a very dumb dog in a dunce hat*.

Jennie giggled as she pulled on her long black dress.

Beth wriggled into her costume. "You look very scary, Sam." She tried not to smile.

Sam just glared.

Beth burst out laughing.

Very funny. I hope you laugh yourself into a big fit.

Beth doubled over and fell on the bed. She laughed so hard, tears streamed down her cheeks. Jennie couldn't stop herself — she broke into a fit of giggles.

Sam glowered at her friends. *If you two think I'm going out on Halloween in this get-up, you've got another thing coming.*

"Sam's not going, Beth."

Beth hooted.

Sam growled.

Then Jennie thought of something. "What about the treats, Sam?" She winked at Beth.

Sam stopped growling instantly. *Yeah ... well ... I forgot about the candy.*

Jennie grinned. "So you'll come?"

Well ... Sam looked hard at Jennie. *You're sure I'm getting a really big bag?*

Jennie laughed. "Here." She pulled out a brown paper shopping bag and set it in front of Sam. "Is this big enough?"

Sam stuck her head into the empty bag. In her mind, she saw it overflowing with candy and bubble gum and caramel popcorn balls. She looked up. *I'll do it*.

Jennie laughed harder. "Guess what, Beth? Sam's going."

Beth grinned lovingly at Sam as she wiped the tears from her eyes. "I kind of thought she would."

Just before bedtime that night, the phone rang. It was Beth.

"Look outside, Jennie."

Jennie looked out her bedroom window. Thick fog was closing in against the glass.

She gulped.

"This fog is so weird." Beth's voice sounded hollow.

Jennie could hear Beth's mother calling her. "I have to go to bed now," Beth said. "Bye."

Jennie looked back at the mist swirling against the window pane. Slithering fear crawled over her skin.

Slowly, Jennie put down the phone.

The next day, Jennie told Sam she was getting very nervous about Halloween.

Don't worry about a thing. Sam chomped down three jelly doughnuts and snuffled in a bag of cheese puffs. *I have wonderful teeth*.

"Forget your wonderful teeth, Sam. These are ghouls!"

Ghouls, shmouls. Who cares? I'll bite them if they come near us.

Sam looked up with icing sugar stuck to her black nose. *Wait a minute. Are these ghouls rotten or anything?*

"I don't think so." Jennie looked at Beth. "Did the book say anything about the ghouls being rotten?"

Beth shook her head. "Nope."

Good. Sam went back to her snack. *I have great teeth, but I don't bite anything rotten.*

Stick with me, and we'll be fine.

7. Sam Looks for Clues

When Sam went out on her front porch that night, she stared into the thick fog and listened. She was sure she heard voices coming from the woods.

The ghouls are getting ready out there. I knew it.

After school, she fixed Jennie with a hard stare. *Halloween is only three days away. We should see some sign of those ghouls.*

"All we've seen is fog." Jennie dipped her nacho into the dip. "And that doesn't mean ghouls are coming."

Something's happening. Sam looked at Jennie long and hard, the hair over her eyes lifting. *I'm a detective. Help me out here.*

"Nothing's happening." Jennie thought for moment. "People are putting up ghosts and spiders and webs and all sorts of scary stuff on their houses."

"I never saw Woodford decorated this much," added Beth.

Oh-ho! So the town's different this year ... That means people know the ghouls are coming. They're getting ready.

Jennie rolled her eyes. "Nobody is getting ready for ghouls."

Sam ignored her. *Did you see anything else? Is anybody acting suspicious?* She stared at Jennie again. *Ask Beth.*

Jennie turned to Beth. "Sam wants to know if we've seen anything suspicious."

Beth was instantly thoughtful. "Well ... only the decorations and the fog ... I guess it's a bit strange at the Catherbys' house."

"The Catherbys'?" Jennie looked surprised.

"Yeah. Those big trunks on the porch," said Beth.

Trunks, eh?

"Those trunks do look strange," admitted Jennie. "They're so big."

Beth nodded. "And a new trunk comes every day."

Sam's head whipped up out of the salsa bowl. *That sounds like a clue!*

"There are four trunks there now."

Hmmm ... Who are the Catherbys?

"The Catherbys are nice — they're old. Beth and I talk to them sometimes on the way home from school."

Do they look like ghouls?

Jennie smiled. "No, they don't look a bit like ghouls. They're really friendly."

Beth smiled, too. "They're definitely not ghouls, Sam. They're ordinary."

Huge trunks aren't ordinary. Sam's mind started to whir. *Why would somebody put a trunk on their porch every day? And why would they do it the week before Halloween?*

She looked up at her friends. *Let's go for a walk. I want to see this.*

Through the dull autumn afternoon, Sam, Jennie and Beth walked the few blocks to the Catherbys'. They passed lawns decorated with tombstones. A skeleton hung from a tree.

Suddenly, Jennie shivered. "I used to like Halloween. But now it looks so spooky."

It's supposed to be spooky.

Beth noticed mist gathering in the distance. "More fog," she muttered.

Jennie squinted down the street at the fog.

The late afternoon light was fading when the girls stopped at a high gate. Sam looked up curiously.

"The Catherbys live there," said Jennie, nodding at a house set back off the road.

Sam put her paws up on the fence and peered at the house. It was an old, red brick house with a wide veranda. Two huge maple trees flanked the front steps. On the porch stood four enormous black trunks.

Hmmm ... Sam sniffed. But she couldn't smell anything interesting. She tried to stretch her neck over the fence. The windows looked dark and empty.

Sam turned to Jennie. *So — where are the Catherbys?*

"Inside I guess," said Jennie.

Sam looked back at the house. *It doesn't look like anybody's home.*

"But they're always there," said Jennie. "Beth and I wave at them every day."

Beth strained to see. "Maybe they're out."

"But they're always home," protested Jennie.

Maybe somebody locked them in the attic. Sam fixed Jennie with a long look. *Or in one of those trunks.*

"Quit saying spooky things!" cried Jennie. "They've probably gone shopping!"

Sam shrugged. *Maybe ... maybe not.*

Mark my words, Jennie.

Something's strange here.

8. Sam Sees the Ghouls

For a long time Jennie, Beth and Sam huddled at the fence watching the Catherbys' house. The afternoon was oddly quiet. Fog thickened around them.

"I've never seen the house empty," mused Beth. "I hope they haven't been kidnapped."

"You sound like Sam," snorted Jennie. "She thinks they're locked up in one of those trunks."

Beth's eyebrows flew up. "Maybe they are!"

Let's rescue them. Sam was nudging at the gate when she heard a car.

Quick! Get behind these bushes. I want to spy.

Sam dove into the bushes, and Jennie and

Beth followed. Very carefully, they peered past the evergreen branches so they could see through the fence into the yard.

A black van was pulling into the Catherbys' driveway.

The three friends stiffened. The van was painted with horrible faces — hooded, white-faced creatures with spiky hair and black, black eyes.

"Look at the side of the van," breathed Jennie.

"Yeah," muttered Beth. "This is weird."

Hmmm . . .

Jennie, Beth and Sam held their breath as the van door opened. Someone stepped out. Its back was to them. Then it turned around.

Jennie whimpered.

Sam gasped. *Yikes!*

Stepping onto the Catherbys' sidewalk was a creature with spiky purple hair, a chalk-white face, black eyes and blood-red lips. It wore a black, studded leather jacket and high boots. Reaching back into the front seat, it brought out a long, black cape and flung it around its shoulders.

It's a ghoul!

Huddled behind the bush, the three friends didn't move.

Out of the van sprang more ghouls. They were all dressed in the same black leather with studs and boots. Their hair was blue and orange and green and pink. Whispering, they hovered near the van. Then the driver pointed to the house.

They're making plans!

One of them sprang up the steps and grabbed the handle of a trunk. Another ghoul ran to the other end.

The creatures didn't say a word. They nodded at each other and carried the trunk to the door.

The ghoul with the cape seemed to be the leader. Pulling a key out, it opened the door and held it wide.

There was no sign of life inside the house.

The fog thickened around Jennie, Beth and Sam. The afternoon was suddenly still.

The ghouls heaved the trunk through the

door into the blackness of the empty doorway.

Above them, the lifeless windows stared.

Then the door shut and they were gone.

9. What's in the Trunks?

Jennie, Beth and Sam stayed behind the bushes and watched. A ghoul came to the window and pulled the curtains shut.

Three teenagers stopped in front of the house and stared.

Sam glared at them.

"What are they doing?" hissed Beth.

Jennie shrugged. "Looks like they're waiting for something."

Did I ever tell you I hate teenagers?

"They're staring at the house." Beth was puzzled.

The teenagers kept pointing at the house and whispering. Then they turned and walked off into the fog.

Jennie, Beth and Sam waited. But nothing happened.

Phooey. We can't spy with the curtains closed.

The afternoon was turning dark.

"I should go home," said Jennie suddenly. "My mom will be worried."

Beth stared hard at the house. "I wonder where Mr. and Mrs. Catherby are."

The ghouls got them.

Just then, the front door opened and two ghouls came out. They picked up a trunk and hoisted it on their shoulders.

Two different ghouls came out and grabbed another trunk.

Hmmm …

Jennie, Beth and Sam watched the ghouls move the trunks inside one by one.

The door shut again, and the three friends were alone. No sound came from the house.

At last, Jennie stood up. "It's almost dark," she whispered. "We better go."

"Yeah," Beth agreed. "My mom hates it if

I'm late for supper."

Sam sighed. *I wish somebody would make me supper. All I ever get is Liver Delight.*

Jennie smiled. "I'll save you something, Sam."

It better be pie or cake or pork chops. Don't try feeding me peas and corn and junk like that.

"I promise, Your Majesty."

Very funny.

Together, they walked home through the deepening twilight. Fog rolled down the streets.

Jennie shivered. "Why does Halloween seem so strange this year?"

Because this is the year. That's why.

Beth chewed her nails as she walked. "It's got something to do with those ghouls."

I heard them talking in the woods.

Jennie gasped. "You heard ghouls talking?"

"She did?" Beth stopped in her tracks.

They've been having meetings in the woods by

the old airfield.

"She says they were in the woods making plans."

Beth's jaw dropped. Jennie chewed her lip.

Sam peered into the fog. *Hey! Have you two noticed that nobody is out driving?*

"We haven't seen any cars, have we, Beth?" Jennie gulped.

Beth shook her head and looked into the fog. "That's so weird."

Sam shuddered. In her mind, she could see ghouls wrapped in black capes sneaking through the fog … on their way from the cemetery … hundreds of them … all looking for children to snatch.

I tell you, Jennie. This is the year.

Jennie shivered. "Sam keeps saying this is the year of the ghouls."

"It sure seems like it." Beth glanced behind her nervously.

Don't worry. I'll bite them.

"Stop saying that!" Jennie stamped her foot. "You might not have a chance to bite them.

Besides," she glared down at her friend, "I've never seen you bite anybody."

No need to be insulting. Sam sniffed. *I was always biting crooks in my old neighborhood. Everybody was scared of me.*

"I bet," snorted Jennie.

Sam shot her a nasty look.

"We know you have wonderful teeth, Sam," said Beth soothingly. "But ghouls are strong."

They fell silent. Fog swirled around them with tiny fingers. The only sound was their footsteps.

At last, Jennie spoke. "You don't really think the Catherbys are locked in one of those trunks, do you?"

Beth shrugged. "I don't know. But I wonder what's in them."

Sam looked up calmly. *You don't want to know. Believe me.*

"What do you think is in them?" Jennie looked down at Sam.

Sam paused. *Remember, I'm the detective here.*

Jennie rolled her eyes. "We know you're

the detective, Sam. So, what's in the trunks?"

You won't like it.

"Just tell me," insisted Jennie.

Sam sat down on the sidewalk. *The trunks are hiding something, right?*

"I guess so." Jennie stopped and turned to look back at Sam.

Of course they are. And the trunks were moved into the house by ghouls, right?

Jennie nodded.

Ghouls look very weird, don't they?

Jennie nodded again. "Very ugly."

Well ... you haven't seen anything yet.

The worst-looking ones are hiding in those trunks.

10. Halloween Night

The days before Halloween grew foggier and foggier. At night, the streetlights cast tiny pools of eerie yellow light into the mist. An odd silence crept over the town.

Twice Jennie, Beth and Sam walked over to the Catherbys'. But the ghouls didn't appear again. The van was gone, and there was no sign of Mr. and Mrs. Catherby.

By the time Halloween night arrived, Jennie was jittery.

"I d-don't think I want to go trick-or-treating this year," she said, when Beth and Sam came over to put on their costumes.

Sam spun around from the mirror. *Are you*

crazy? Think of the candy! The witch hat slid sideways over one ear.

Jennie pulled off her hat and let her costume fall to the floor. "I'm not crazy. Think of the ghouls."

Sam glared. *Did I ever tell you how much I hate wimps!*

"I know you hate w-wimps." Jennie's lip trembled. "But I'm t-too scared to go."

Beth stopped putting on makeup. "We can't stay home, Jennie! We'll miss all the fun!"

"It wouldn't be any fun being a ghoul," muttered Jennie.

"We won't get turned into ghouls!" cried Beth. "Sam will protect us."

Yeah. I have wonderful —

Jennie glared at Sam. "Don't say a word about your stupid teeth!"

Maybe I'll bite you. Sam glared back, the witch hat hanging under her chin.

Beth and I are going. Sam nudged Beth's leg with her nose. *Tell Beth to fix this dumb hat. We're out of here.*

"I don't want to go without you. Come on, Jennie. It'll be so much fun!" Beth fixed Sam's hat and cape.

"Some fun," groaned Jennie. "Being a ghoul and sleeping in a cemetery."

Stop whining. Sam clamped her teeth on Beth's dress and pulled her toward the door.

But Beth turned back to Jennie. "Please come, Jennie," she begged. "We'll be careful."

I'm not sharing my loot with wimps. Sam picked up the bag in her teeth and shoved her way out the bedroom door.

Jennie jumped off the bed and jammed the witch hat on her head. "I can't stay here by myself. That's even scarier!"

Now we're getting somewhere. Sam danced down the stairs toward the front door.

Halloween, here we come!

When they opened the front door, they stepped into swirling fog. They couldn't see down the street, but they could hear voices.

Out of the fog loomed a grinning monster. Jennie screamed. The face disappeared.

Relax. It's only a kid out trick-or-treating.

"How are w-we g-going to be careful when we can't see anything?"

I can smell ghouls. Trust me.

"How do you know what they smell like?"

They hang around cemeteries, don't they? I can smell a cemetery anywhere.

Jennie thought about this for a moment, then she relaxed a bit. "Do you think Sam will be able to smell the ghouls?" she asked, as they stumbled along.

"Sure." Beth was cheerful. "Why didn't we think of that? Dogs have terrific noses."

"And wonderful teeth," giggled Jennie.

"I'm glad you're a dog, Sam," said Beth. "Just keep sniffing."

Sam lifted her head proudly and sniffed the air. *No ghouls around. Now for the candy.*

They made their way down the street, ringing doorbell after doorbell. People gooed and gushed when they saw Sam.

"What a wonderful witch you are, pretty doggie," one lady cried.

Just hand over the candy, lady.

"What an adorable dog!" burbled another.

Of course, I'm adorable. Smart, too. Don't forget smart.

Kids squealed and clapped their hands. "Can we get a dog like this one? Please, Mom."

If they keep feeding me Liver Delight at Joan and Bob's, I'll move in with you, kid. Now, get the candy.

After they left each house, Sam stopped at the end of the walk, set down the bag and looked inside. If she found a granola bar or an apple, she grabbed it with her teeth and dropped it into Jennie's bag.

Believe me, I'm not dressed in this ridiculous outfit to get healthy junk. I want candy.

Then she led the way through the fog to the next house.

The night was seething with monsters. Skeletons, vampires and aliens loomed out of the fog. Each face was a shock.

Every once in a while, Sam sniffed the air. *No ghouls*, she announced happily. After an hour even Jennie forgot about the ghouls and had fun.

"I'm glad you decided to come, Jennie," giggled Beth as they crossed the street.

"Me, too." Jennie looked down at Sam carrying her bag in her teeth. "Don't forget to keep sniffing, Sam."

No problem.

At the end of the street Sam suddenly sat down with a thud. *Did you hear those kids talking about the Catherbys?*

Jennie nodded. "They said the Catherbys are giving out giant chocolate bars."

I want one. Let's go.

"We are not going to the Catherbys'!" Jennie gasped. "Are you crazy? That's where the ghouls are!"

Sam glared. *Are we going to have another one*

of your famous wimp-outs?

"Sam, the ghouls are there!" cried Jennie desperately. "You saw them!"

We'll get the chocolate bar and run.

"It's too dangerous!"

We're going. Sam stared hard. *I'm getting a giant chocolate bar. And no one's going to stop me.*

Sam disappeared into the fog.

11. The Scariest House in Woodford

"I hate that dog sometimes," muttered Jennie, as she and Beth stumbled after Sam.

"Sam! Wait!" Jennie cried. "She's t-taking us to the g-ghouls, Beth!"

"Don't worry," puffed Beth. "They don't grab any kids until midnight. And we've got Sam to protect us."

"Someday that dog is going to get us killed!" panted Jennie.

They stopped at Main Street, where the streetlights cast an eerie glow into the misty dark. Bright neon signs flicked on and off in the fog.

"I can't see anybody," whispered Jennie.

“That’s because everybody’s trick-or-treating.”

“There she is!” cried Jennie, as she saw Sam disappear into an alley across the street. “She’s taking the shortcut to the Catherbys’!”

“Let’s go!” Beth darted after Sam with Jennie right behind her.

In moments, they came out on the Catherbys’ street. Sam was waiting in a misty pool of light under a street lamp.

Hurry up. The chocolate bars will be gone.

And Sam dashed down the street.

“This is not smart,” Jennie muttered over and over, as they followed Sam down the foggy street.

When they stopped in front of the Catherbys’ gate, Jennie’s mouth felt dry, and her hands were sweaty. “This is definitely not smart,” she repeated.

The gates were open. But there were no

trick-or-treaters coming out of the house, and no one seemed to be around.

Gulping, Jennie and Beth looked at the two huge trees hanging over the porch. Beside the door, a fierce jack-o'-lantern shimmered, and a dim light shone through one of the upstairs windows.

"It looks kind of dark," whispered Jennie.

Who cares? Sam trotted up the walk. *This is where the chocolate bars are. Come on.*

Jennie and Beth clutched each other.

"Are you sure we should do this?" Jennie asked, her heart thumping in her throat.

"We have to stay with Sam," whispered Beth. "We're safe with her."

"Okay," breathed Jennie. "We'll stand behind Sam while she gets that stupid chocolate bar. Then we'll run as fast as we can."

"Don't you want one?" Beth sounded surprised.

"I just want to get out of here."

"I guess you're right." Beth started up the walk after Sam. "Let's get this over with."

Jennie followed her friends, her footsteps swishing through the dry leaves. A sudden wind rattled the tree branches overhead with a ghostly sound.

The floorboards creaked when they crossed the porch to the front door. As if it were laughing, the jack-o'-lantern flickered at them.

Taking a deep breath, Beth reached up and knocked.

Nothing happened.

She knocked again, her knuckles making a hollow sound in the still air.

Nothing.

They waited.

I told you those chocolate bars would be gone.

Then, with a blood-curdling scream, the house burst into life!

Jennie and Beth froze.

The front door swung open, and a bleeding head on a stick floated out. Fiendish laughter filled the air. Gravestones popped up on the front lawn. Horrible faces sprang to life in every window.

Loud screaming whirled around them like a tornado. The cackling was horrible.

Beth screamed, looking wildly for a place to hide.

"We've got you now!" shrieked a voice from the trees. From somewhere else came high-pitched giggles.

"Come to mama, you tasty little morsel," croaked a voice from a window.

"Help!" screamed Beth, grabbing Jennie.

"Woof!" barked Sam. "Grrrrrr. Woof!" *Watch it ghouls. I'll bite off your toes!*

"Grrrr."

Suddenly, the laughter stopped. Rising and falling like a demon in a deep pit, a ghostly moan filled the air. On and on it went, telling of dark nights and terrible secrets that no human should ever know.

Jennie and Beth started to shake.

"You are mine now, my sweeties," moaned a new voice from the house.

Hmph. I guess this means no chocolate bar.

12. Hiding from the Ghouls

Beth tugged Jennie's arm. "Quick! Hide!" She pointed to some bushes beside the porch.

When Jennie didn't move, Beth yanked her off the porch into the bushes. "We have to hide!" she hissed.

Sam jumped off the porch and wedged herself in beside the girls, just as a new voice echoed out of the trees. "Come here, my pretties! I have you now!"

Jennie, Beth and Sam wriggled flat on their stomachs under the bushes. They held their breath and waited. A long, low growl rumbled deep in Sam's throat.

"Be quiet, Sam," whispered Jennie. "They'll

find us!"

Sam clamped her mouth shut.

"Get down!" hissed Beth. "Don't move."

Who made her the boss?

They waited, hearts pounding, their faces in the dirt.

Then they heard it. A new kind of laughter was spilling out the front door. It sounded human.

Hey! Ghouls can sound like people.

"Did you see those kids run!" chortled one voice.

"Funniest thing I've ever seen!" laughed another.

"Where did they go?" asked a third voice.

Then all three ghouls whooped with laughter. They laughed and laughed until they hiccuped.

I hope you split your ghoulie sides.

When they finally stopped laughing, there was a long silence. Under the bushes, Jennie, Beth and Sam tensed.

"Did you see that stupid-looking dog?" chuckled a ghoul. "That thing was the biggest chicken of all!"

Watch it, ghouls. I'm a very tough dog and I don't like insults.

Sam breathed dirt into her nose. *I'm getting grumpy. My beautiful fur is getting dirty. And this dumb witch hat is choking me.*

Beth and Jennie could hardly breathe. The ghouls' footsteps moved closer to the edge of the porch.

Just when Jennie was sure the ghouls would look down and see them, one of them said, "Forget the kids. Let's go over to the high school."

They want teenagers. Good. I hate teenagers.

"I guess it's okay. There doesn't seem to be any more trick-or-treaters around," said another ghoul.

"We might as well go to the high school and set up."

Did you hear that, Jennie? They're setting traps at the high school!

Jennie didn't answer. Her heart was hammering in her chest. The three friends lay stone still until the footsteps went back into the house.

The front door clicked shut.

13. Who's This?

No one moved.

After a few moments, the three friends heard doors slam. An engine started at the back of the house. Sam raised her head and watched the headlights back out of the driveway.

"Get down, Sam," hissed Jennie. "They might see you."

Nobody can see in this fog.

"Maybe one of the ghouls is still here!"

They listened, but there was nothing to hear. The house was quiet — as if it were waiting for something.

Sam poked her head up and sniffed. *Nobody's here.*

Just as Jennie was about to ask if Sam was sure, headlights swept over the lawn.

Yikes! They're back!

Jennie, Beth and Sam ducked.

But the headlights stopped on the street in front of the gate. A car door opened. Through the mist, they could see two shapes getting out of the car. Then the shapes turned around and reached in the back seat for something.

They heard muttered voices, a car door closing and the car pulling away. Two shapes carrying bags came up the walk.

So, who's this?

Mutter. Mutter.

It's someone else. They're talking about a trip.

Mutter. Mutter.

As the voices got closer, the girls could hear what they said.

"I certainly hope we haven't missed all the fun."

It was Mrs. Catherby!

14. The Catherbys Return

Still chatting, Mr. and Mrs. Catherby carried their suitcases up the porch steps. Jennie, Beth and Sam heard the key turn in the front door.

"I hope we get some trick-or-treaters," said Mr. Catherby, as the front door swung open.

"I had no idea we'd be this late," said Mrs. Catherby.

Then the front door closed, and their voices got fainter.

Under the bushes, the three friends waited until they couldn't hear any more.

Peeking up over the edge of the porch, Sam sniffed. The fog was so thick, she couldn't see the street. She sniffed again. Nobody was around.

She hopped up on the porch, her tattered witch hat and cape hanging off one side. Stepping on her hat, she went over to the door and listened.

She looked back at Jennie. *You can come out. They're going upstairs.*

"It's safe now, Beth," said Jennie.

Jennie and Beth hauled themselves out of the bushes, pulling twigs and bits of leaves off their costumes. Both their witch hats were gone.

I'm going to warn the Catherbys that ghouls have taken over their house.

"What does Sam hear?" whispered Beth.

"They're upstairs, and she wants to warn them about the ghouls," Jennie whispered back.

"Sam's right!" Beth's eyes widened. "When the ghouls come back, Mr. and Mrs. Catherby will be trapped!"

Sam stepped on the edge of her cape and pulled. *Get this thing off me!* Then she lowered her chin and tried to chew the hat off. *I can't do detective work with this junk hanging all over me!*

As soon as Jennie untied the knots, Sam

shook herself. *Clothes drive me crazy*.

She glared at the door. *I've got to get in*.

"But there might be a ghoul in there!" Jennie looked around the porch anxiously.

All I can hear is the Catherbys.

As Sam stood listening, she suddenly noticed something she hadn't seen before. There was a pet door in the front door panel, the kind that opened when a pet squeezed through it.

Well, well, well ...

See you. Sam shoved her head through the pet door. *I'm going to be a hero.*

Sam could see the newspaper headlines: BRAVE DOG SAVES ELDERLY COUPLE. She smiled to herself as she pictured reporters, TV interviews, talk shows ...

"Sam!" Jennie grabbed Sam's back leg. "Get back here!"

Annoyed, Sam stopped thinking about being a hero. *No way*. Sam yanked her leg through the pet door.

Jennie stuck her head in the opening. "Sam!

Come back!" she hissed. She reached in through the door, but Sam was gone.

"Let's go after her," said Beth. She tried to squeeze her shoulders through the door, but it was too small.

She backed out and sank to the porch floor with a thud. "Sam is a bad dog."

"She sure is! We're never taking her with us on Halloween again," muttered Jennie.

She leaned down and whispered into the pet door again. "Sam!" But there was no answer.

She sat back on her heels beside Beth. "What do we do now?"

15. Inside the House

Hmmm . . . What have we here?

Sam looked around the old-fashioned entrance hall. To her left, a carved staircase led upstairs. To her right, wooden doors opened into a cozy living room.

I think I'll check the place out.

Overhead, the Catherbys were walking back and forth. Drawers were opening and closing. *Sounds like they're unpacking.*

So the Catherbys have been away, and ghouls moved into their house. Very suspicious. Very weird. Sam's mind began to whir. *This is a good case for a smart detective like me.*

She sniffed at the couch and chairs. *Nothing interesting here.*

Outside, Jennie and Beth crouched miserably on the porch. The fog was getting thicker, and there wasn't a sound from the street.

"I d-don't think I like Halloween anymore," gulped Jennie.

"I like it," muttered Beth. "But this one's not turning out."

"We have to get Sam out of there," said Jennie.

"We will," said Beth. "But why can't we hear anything?"

Jennie swallowed hard. "Maybe the ghouls got her."

The girls wanted to go home, but they couldn't go without Sam. They crouched silently ... waiting ... watching ...

"Maybe she'll come out by herself," said

Jennie at last.

"Yeah. So we can wring her neck," muttered Beth.

Sam turned to look into the dining room and stopped in her tracks.

Uh-oh.

In the dining room, stacked against the wall, were the four huge trunks she'd seen on the porch.

I wonder if ghouls are still hiding in those trunks ... or did they leave with their friends?

Hmmm ...

Suddenly, Sam's nose caught a whiff of something wonderful. Instantly, all thoughts of the ghouls flew out of her head. *Chocolate! That's what I came for!*

Sam followed the smell past the trunks into the kitchen. *Yum.* Sniff. Sniff. *Yum. Yum.* She looked around curiously.

Dishes littered the table. On the counters stood open pizza boxes, take-out chicken buckets, old pop cans and spilled boxes of cereal. *Wow. It's a feast in here.*

Sam snuffled at the edge of the counter. Around the kitchen she went, sniffing, sniffing. ... *Pizza ... toast and jam ... eggs ... pancakes ... I think I have time for a little snack ...* Through all the delicious smells, the lovely odor of chocolate tickled Sam's nose. She licked her chops.

Sam looked around for something to stand on.

Her gaze landed on a bar with some electrical cords plugged into it. Following the cords, Sam saw that they ran under the kitchen window to the outside.

What's this?

Still sniffing, Sam walked over to the power bar and looked closely at it. At one end was a switch.

Hmmm ... This is interesting ...

I wonder what it is ...

Sam reached out her paw and pressed the switch.

16. Jennie's Worst Nightmare

With an ear-splitting scream, the house burst into life again!

Jennie and Beth covered their heads.

The front door flung open! A bleeding head on a stick floated out! Laughter echoed through the fog. Gravestones popped up on the lawn and cackling faces lit up the windows.

Jennie and Beth screamed.

"We've got you now!" shrieked the voice from the trees. Ghoulish giggling echoed over the old porch.

When they heard, "Come to mama, you tasty little morsel," they grabbed each other.

"It's the ghouls!" cried Jennie. "They've got us!"

Inside, Sam reeled as the house erupted! Screams howled all around her. Cackling shrieked out of the walls. Voices wailed through the rooms.

This can't be good.

In her mind, Sam saw the lids of the trunks opening in the dining room. Horrible ghouls were climbing out — worse than anything Sam had ever seen. Their faces were filthy from the cemeteries. Stinking grave clothes dragged behind them, dirt stained, reeking of death.

Sam gulped. *Maybe they're mad about something.*

A sudden thought hit her. *I know what they're mad about. It's me! They know I'm in here!*

In a flash, Sam squeezed under the kitchen table and curled up in a ball. *Maybe they'll think I'm a rug.*

The house rattled with screams and echoes and terrible, terrible laughter.

Then Sam had a new thought. *They're sure laughing a lot. Maybe they've got Jennie and Beth!* Her heart sank.

I can't stay here while they kidnap my friends. Watch out, you ghouls. I've got wonderful teeth ...

Teeth that scare everybody.

"Run!" screeched Beth, as a new voice moaned at them from the fog. "We've got to hide!"

She grabbed Jennie and pulled her down the steps and across the front of the house.

All around them the moaning rose and fell like the screams of the dead. When they got to the backyard they looked wildly around at the mist.

"Behind the garage!" yelled Beth.

Stumbling through the fog, the girls made their way to the back of the garage and crouched down beside a woodpile.

"You are mine now, my sweeties," moaned a voice from the house.

Jennie and Beth were frozen with terror.

17. The Ghouls Are Back!

As suddenly as it started, all the screaming and giggling and laughing stopped. Silence fell over the house again.

Whew! Sam peeked out from under the tablecloth.

Baring her fangs, she growled a deep menacing growl. "Grrrr ..."

Just as she was crawling out from under the table, bright lights flashed through the kitchen window. *Uh-oh!*

Headlights swept across the wall. Someone was pulling into the driveway!

Sam backed under the table.

Car doors slammed. Voices were coming

toward the house.

Maybe it's the cops. Maybe they heard about these ghouls.

But as she listened, her heart sank. She knew those voices.

It's the ghouls! They're back!

Outside, Jennie and Beth held on to each other as the bright headlights swept over the driveway.

Shrinking down, they waited as car doors opened and shut. As soon as they heard the voices, they knew who it was!

"The ghouls!" gulped Beth.

In horror, they listened as the ghouls crunched up the gravel driveway to the back door.

"They'll c-catch Sam!" whispered Jennie frantically.

"They'll take her to the forest." Beth's heart sank.

"P-poor Sam!" Jennie's voice broke.

Beth gritted her teeth. "We'll get her out."

Jennie blinked back tears.

Just then the back door opened. A triangle of light glistened on the mist. Jennie and Beth could see the ghouls' weird shapes trooping into the house.

The kitchen door closed and the yard was dark and silent again.

"Now we'll hear them grab Sam." Beth scrunched her eyes shut.

Jennie held her breath. But no sound came from the house.

Under the table, Sam heard snatches of conversation as the ghouls trooped into the kitchen.

"I don't know where I put it."

"Maybe you left it on the counter."

Left what? Their last victim, maybe. I bet they

chewed him up and he's in one of those chicken containers.

"We've got to find it fast and get back to the high school," said the first ghoul.

"They're in for a big surprise tonight!" another ghoul chortled happily.

Stop talking about your crummy surprises. I want Jennie and Beth back.

While the ghouls shuffled around the kitchen opening drawers and cupboards, Sam stayed hidden under the table. All she could see from under the edge of the tablecloth were huge black boots.

She hated being so close to the ghouls. Without realizing it, she bared her fangs and a low growl started deep in her throat.

Don't try to grab me, ghouls.

I'm ready for you!

18. To the Rescue

"There's got to be a way to save Sam," Beth hissed.

Jennie just sniffled.

"I've got it!" Beth stood up and wiped the dirt from her witch dress. "We'll go to the door and pretend we're trick-or-treating. Come on."

"How w-will that s-save her?" stammered Jennie.

"She'll hear us and run out." Beth started around the woodpile.

Jennie's stomach heaved. They would be face-to-face with the ghouls.

"Hurry," hissed Beth. "We need to get there before they shove her in a trunk."

Jennie scurried to catch up as Beth disappeared into the fog.

"The Catherbys can run outside, too," whispered Beth, as they sneaked around the side of the house.

She stopped suddenly. "We need our witch hats."

The girls crept to the side of the porch. Beth groped in the bushes for the hats, and handed one to Jennie.

Jennie rammed it on. A tattered piece of bristol board hung from the peak. "These are wrecked," she whispered.

"Who cares?" muttered Beth. "We're trick-or-treaters. That's all that matters."

Hearts pounding, Jennie and Beth started up the porch steps to the front door.

Beth tugged at Jennie's arm. "Remember the little boy in the story," she hissed. "We have to pretend we're not scared of them."

Slowly, they crossed the porch.

They had to get Sam.

The minute Beth rang the doorbell, the house burst into life again!

Hands over their ears, Jennie and Beth clung to each other as the bleeding head floated out the door, and the air filled with cackles and shrieks and moans.

Under the kitchen table, Sam heard the doorbell ring. The black boots moving around the kitchen stopped.

Instantly the house filled with the same shrieking screams and moans she'd heard before.

"Trick-or-treaters!" exclaimed one of the ghouls happily.

All the black boots ran out of the kitchen.

"It's the same every time," cried Beth. "See?" She pointed to the horrible faces leering from the windows. "Nothing else will happen."

Jennie didn't feel so sure. Maybe it was a trick so the ghouls could grab kids, and nobody would hear them scream. She shrank back from the door.

A ghoul suddenly peeked around the open doorway. White face, blood-red lips and black-rimmed eyes leered at them.

"Well, well, well," he said licking his lips. "What have we here?"

19. Tricking the Ghouls

Jennie and Beth gasped as four more ghouls appeared in the doorway. Where was Sam? Why didn't she run out?

"Yes, indeed," the ghouls cried. "Trick-or-treaters at last."

"Ha! Ha! Ha!" shrieked Beth, pulling her lips back in a wild grin.

The ghouls looked at her oddly.

"Happy Halloween!" the purple-haired ghoul said, rubbing his hands together.

Jennie was spellbound by those rubbing hands. He looked like he was waiting for a nice piece of roast dog.

Rub. Rub. Rub. "I love trick-or-treaters,"

he crooned.

Jennie gulped. Maybe he was thinking of roast trick-or-treater!

Beth threw back her head and laughed crazily. "Ha! Ha! Ha!" she screamed again.

The ghouls looked at one another in surprise.

The orange-haired one shrugged. "Maybe it's supposed to be a witch laugh."

"Ha! Ha! Ha!" Beth squawked again. She whirled to Jennie who was frozen against the porch railing. "Funny, huh, Jennie? Ha! Ha!"

All the ghouls leaned out the door and stared at Beth.

"What a weird kid," the green-haired ghoul muttered.

Beth grinned up at them like a jack-o'-lantern.

"Maybe the kid thinks witches laugh all the time," said the blue-haired ghoul.

Suddenly, Beth stopped grinning and yelled into the doorway at the top of her lungs. "Sam! Run!"

The ghouls stepped back in amazement.

“Who’s Sam?” the pink-haired ghoul asked.

“What’s the matter with this kid?” asked another.

“None of your business!” yelled Beth. “Sam!” she screamed, the veins standing out on her neck.

All the ghouls looked around the entrance hall. “Who’s Sam?” repeated the purple-haired ghoul.

“Nobody!” screamed Beth. “Ha! Ha! Ha! Sam!”

Under the table, Sam gasped in surprise. Beth was calling her!

But Sam didn’t move. *Beth’s lost her mind! I can’t go out with ghouls all over the place.*

Just then Sam noticed the bottom of the back door. *Maybe I could get out that way . . .*

She peeked out from under the tablecloth and looked around the empty kitchen.

Carefully, she sneaked over to the kitchen door and picked at it with her paw. It was shut tight. She bit down on the doorknob and tried to twist it, but her teeth slid off.

"Sam!" It was Beth again, screaming at the top of her lungs.

Shut up, Beth.

"Sam!" Now Jennie was calling, too.

Don't they know it's not safe to call me? Sam sighed. *I have very stupid friends.*

Sam stopped chewing the doorknob. *Wait a minute! Why are Jennie and Beth screaming when they know there are ghouls around?*

Uh-oh. This must be a trick. The ghouls have kidnapped Jennie and Beth. They're forcing the girls to call me.

Sam growled deep in her throat.

You can't fool me, ghouls.

Your tricks won't work on the world's best detective!

20. The Catherbys Come Downstairs

Just as Beth opened her mouth to laugh again, something moved on the stairway.

Down the stairs scurried the Catherbys. They jammed into the doorway beside the ghouls.

"Why, it's Jennie and Beth!" exclaimed Mrs. Catherby. "What a lovely surprise!"

Jennie opened her mouth to warn the old couple. "Ugh … Aaaah …" But no words came out.

"Run!" screamed Beth at the Catherbys. "You too, Sam!" she screeched into the doorway.

"What on earth is the matter?" cried Mr. Catherby in surprise.

"Who's Sam?" asked Mrs. Catherby.

"Sam's our dog!" cried Beth. "They've got her!" She pointed at the ghouls.

Mrs. Catherby raised her eyebrows. "They have!" She looked accusingly at the ghouls.

The purple-haired ghoul looked offended. "We don't know any Sam."

"What's all this about?" Mr. Catherby demanded.

Beth looked at the Catherbys closely. They didn't look frightened. Maybe that's why they were safe. "Ha! Ha! Ha!" she screeched.

"Do you feel all right, dear?" Mrs. Catherby asked, with a worried frown.

"I'm fine! I'm good! I'm great! I'm having a wonderful Halloween!" screamed Beth. "Ha! Ha! Ha!" she added, just to be sure the ghouls knew she wasn't scared.

The Catherbys looked at each other in bewilderment.

Mrs. Catherby shrugged. "Too much sugar affects some children ..." Her voice trailed off in puzzlement.

Beth didn't notice. "We know you've got her trapped in there!" she shouted at the ghouls.

The ghouls raised their painted eyebrows. "We do?"

"Sam!" screeched Beth as loud as she could.

Suddenly, Jennie sprang to life. "Sam! Come out here!" she yelled.

Mr. and Mrs. Catherby narrowed their eyes and looked suspiciously at Jennie and Beth.

Then they turned their gaze on the ghouls.

"Hey! Don't look at me!" exclaimed the purple-haired ghoul.

"These kids are crazy!"

21. Sam to the Rescue

Hand them over, ghouls! Here I come.

Sam trotted toward the dining room. Holding her breath, she peered slowly around the door frame. A long, low growl rumbled deep in her throat.

In the dining room, the trunks were closed. But Sam wasn't fooled. She knew they were empty. *Ugh*. She shuddered. *The ugly ghouls are out running around now*.

This is dangerous stuff. Good thing I'm not a wimp. She remembered the little boy in the story who wasn't afraid of the ghouls. *That's me. I'll be so brave they'll never touch me*.

But a dog can't laugh. She thought for a

moment. *I know. I'll growl instead. Growling is good.*

"Gr-r-r-r-r-r-r-r." Sam tiptoed through the dining room past the trunks.

"Gr-r-r-r-r," she crept through the empty living room. No one was there. Very quietly she moved toward the voices at the front door.

When Sam got to the entrance hall, she reeled in shock. All the ghouls stood in the doorway with their backs to her. A white-haired man and woman were with them, looking out at something on the porch.

Oh-ho! So that's it! The ugly ones are on the porch. And they've captured Jennie and Beth.

Sam sneaked up behind the ghouls.

The ghouls were still looking out on the porch.

Sam bared her teeth. *Watch out for the teeth, ghouls!*

Still the ghouls didn't notice.

A growl started deep in Sam's throat. "Gr-r-r-r-r-rrr."

No one seemed to hear.

Sam jumped around in little circles and snapped at their backs. *Watch it ghouls! Back off!* "Woof!" *Very tough dog here!* "Gr-r-r-r-r-r!"

The ghouls turned around.

22. Sam's Wonderful Teeth

"Is this Sam?" asked the blue-haired ghoul.

"Gr-r-r-r-r!" Sam snapped at the air and snarled. *I'm not scared, ghoulies. Out of my way*. "Gr-r-r-r."

The ghouls shrank back. "Stop that!" one of them cried.

Whirling around, Sam snapped and growled and snarled. *Watch it, ghouls! I'm not going to warn you again*. "Gr-r-r-r."

"Man, that's a horrible dog!" cried the pink-haired ghoul.

Hand over my friends. "Gr-r-r-r. Woof!"

The ghouls clustered together. The Catherbys held on to each other.

Okay, that's it! Don't say I didn't warn you!

"If this dog is yours, get it out of here!" cried the blue-haired ghoul.

"Run, Sam!" yelled Jennie.

"No candy for you, dog," shouted the purple-haired ghoul.

"No candy for anybody!" yelled the pink-haired ghoul. These kids are crazy, and the dog is even crazier!"

Watch who you call crazy! Sam grabbed hold of the ghoul's pant leg.

"Our dog is not crazy!" screamed Beth.

"Oh no?" hollered the pink-haired ghoul, shaking Sam off its leg.

"Gr-r-r-r. Woof!" Sam yanked at the pant leg.

"Get off me!" yelled the ghoul.

"This dog must have rabies!" screeched the blue-haired ghoul.

I'm tough and you're toast! Sam went back to work on the ghoul's pants. "Gr-r-r-r-r."

"Somebody call the dog catcher!" yelled the green-haired ghoul.

Sam stopped pulling. *Dog catcher! No way,*

bug face.

"Jennie! Beth!" yelled Mr. Catherby over the din. "Call your dog!"

"Gr-r-r-r-r-r." Sam did three big leaps into the air and dove at the next pant leg.

"Sam!" yelled Jennie. "Come out here!"

Not yet, Jennie. I'll finish these guys off and then I'll get the ugly ones on the porch.

Puzzled, Jennie looked around at the empty porch.

"Jennie, call your dog again!" cried Mrs. Catherby. "This is very scary!"

You bet I'm scary, lady. Watch this. Sam did several little jumps and chomped her teeth in the air. *Good one, huh?*

"Sam!" cried Jennie again. "There are no ghouls out here!"

Look around, Jennie. The ugly ones got out of the trunks.

Jennie looked around. "There's nobody on the porch, Sam. Come out!"

Beth looked up at the ghouls' angry faces. "Ha! Ha! Ha!" she bellowed.

"Somebody get these horrible kids out of here!" roared the green-haired ghoul.

Mrs. Catherby was shaking her head. "I don't understand. Beth and Jennie are usually such nice children."

"I've had it!" shouted the purple-haired ghoul. "Help me grab this stupid mutt!"

All five ghouls jumped on Sam. She felt like she'd been hit by a truck.

Oof!

Wrestling her to the ground, the ghouls held Sam down.

"Don't hurt her!" screamed Beth. "Ha! Ha! Ha!"

"All right, you kids," panted the purple-haired ghoul. "Nobody leaves until we find out what this is all about."

23. Meet the Ghouls

"Tell us," said Mrs. Catherby, folding her arms. "What's wrong with you?"

Mr. Catherby led Jennie and Beth into the living room. "Now, sit down and explain what all this is about."

He looked over at the ghouls holding Sam. "Don't let go of that dog until she behaves."

Sam snorted. *Watch out, Jennie. He's one of them!*

Jennie took a long hard look at Mr. Catherby. *You think they're a nice old couple. I think they're ghouls in disguise.*

Sam craned her neck to look around. *Where are the hideous ones from the trunks?*

Jennie chewed her lip. Beside her Beth was chomping on a fingernail. Both girls were white-faced and nervous.

"What's going on?" demanded Mr. Catherby.

"I've never seen such strange behavior," added Mrs. Catherby.

Jennie and Beth squirmed.

Watch it, Jennie! They're ghouls. Remember?

Jennie jumped up. "We have to go home!" she shouted. "It's late!"

"Just a minute," said Mr. Catherby firmly. "Tell us what's the matter."

"It's the ghouls," answered Beth.

"Ghouls!" Mr. and Mrs. Catherby both looked surprised. "What ghouls?"

Oh, sure. Act innocent.

Jennie and Beth looked over at the ghouls.

Mr. Catherby's eyebrows shot up. "You mean our grandson and his friends?"

Nice try. Very tricky.

"Grandson?" repeated Jennie and Beth together.

The purple-haired ghoul put up his hand.

"That's me."

"This is Jeff," said Mrs. Catherby. "And these boys are his friends."

Like we believe that.

"Boys?" echoed Jennie stupidly.

"We thought they were ghouls," said Beth.

They are ghouls.

Jennie looked up sharply. "They look like ghouls."

"They're supposed to!" Mrs. Catherby exclaimed. "They're dressed up for the big Halloween show at the high school."

The lies never stop.

"Show?" said Jennie.

Beth squinted suspiciously up at Mrs. Catherby. "But they were dressed up days ago!"

Yeah. You can't fool us.

The purple-haired ghoul named Jeff grinned. "We're advertising the show. That's why we painted our van."

Oh, sure.

Sam rolled her eyes at Jennie. *How come they were here all alone?*

"Why were they in the house when you weren't here?" asked Jennie politely.

Mrs. Catherby laughed. "They needed somewhere to practice. We went away on a little trip and let the boys use our house. Jeff's mother can't stand listening to the band anymore!"

All lies.

"B-band?" repeated Jennie, blinking.

"A music group, dear." Mrs. Catherby smiled proudly at her grandson. "They're doing a spooky concert tonight at the high school."

Hey! Remember me? Does anybody care that I'm getting squished down here.

"Can Sam get up, please?" asked Jennie timidly.

"Well . . ." Mrs. Catherby looked suspiciously at Sam. ". . . if she behaves."

Phooey. I always behave.

The ghouls let Sam go. Lumbering to her feet, Sam shook herself and glared at them. *Hmph. Try that again, creeps and —*

"Sam." Jennie's voice was a warning.

Okay, okay.

Sam plopped down beside Jennie. *So what's in the trunks?*

"Excuse me," Jennie asked. "Can you tell us what's in the trunks?"

"Instruments, of course," said Jeff, shaking his spiky purple hair. "What did you think was in them?"

Jennie and Beth looked at each other. Then they looked at the ghouls.

Then they both glared down at Sam.

"What did you think was in the trunks?" repeated the pink-haired ghoul.

"More ghouls," Beth whispered miserably.

All the ghouls laughed.

Very funny.

"I'm curious about something," said Mr. Catherby, leaning toward the girls. "Why did you laugh like that?"

"Well," gulped Beth. "I read this story …" And she told them the legend of the ghouls.

"No wonder you were scared!" cried Mrs. Catherby. "What a dreadful story!"

Even the ghouls nodded their spiky heads. "Very scary."

Sam yawned as everyone talked about the ghoul legend. *Yakkety-yak. I'm getting bored here.*

Come on, Jennie. If there's no mystery in this dump, let's go find one.

I hate the way humans waste time.

24. Sam Makes a New Friend

"Sam was just trying to protect her friends!" Mrs. Catherby smiled kindly at Sam. "She's a beautiful dog!"

You bet, lady. Very beautiful.

Sam glared at Jennie. *I'm not having any fun here, in case anybody cares.*

"And brave!" added Mrs. Catherby.

Absolutely. Very brave.

"Well," said the orange-haired ghoul, "I guess you kids can have candy after all."

Sam's head whipped up. *That's better.*

"We used to have a retriever named Mitzie," said Mr. Catherby. "That's why we have the pet door."

Mrs. Catherby patted Sam's big head. "Our Mitzie used to love a little bedtime snack."

Sam raised a tufty eyebrow. *Sounds sensible.*

Mrs. Catherby giggled. "Mitzie used to eat the strangest things! Her favorite was bologna with ketchup and butterscotch sauce."

Sam licked her lips. *What's so strange about that?*

"And banana and jam sandwiches!" laughed Mrs. Catherby.

Sam stood up and looked hopefully at the kitchen. *I think I love these people. Who said they were ghouls?*

"Come on, Sam." Mrs. Catherby stood up. "I'm going to make you a nice snack. You were a smart dog to protect your friends."

Glad you noticed. Smart, tough, and beautiful. That's me.

"And now you're hungry, aren't you?"

Sure am.

Mrs. Catherby started toward the kitchen. "I'll make you three of Mitzie's favorites."

Just what a clever dog like me deserves. Sam

followed Mrs. Catherby.

In the dining room, she turned and looked back at Jennie. *I think I'll move in here for a while.*

Tell Joan and Bob I don't know when I'll be home.

Read the Sam: Dog Detective series and get set for funny, fast-paced mysteries, featuring the adventures of friends Jennie, Beth and Sam, the sheepdog sleuth!

Spying on Dracula

Ten-year-old Jennie Levinsky has a secret — and only her best friend, Beth, knows about it. Jennie can "hear" what her new neighbor's sheepdog, Sam, is thinking! And what Sam is thinking leads the girls into an exciting adventure at the spookiest house in town. Why is the house always dark? Why is a bat always hanging around? And who is that frightening creature living inside?

The Ghost of Captain Briggs

Jennie and Beth are all set to enjoy their summer vacation with Sam. But how could they know that the house Jennie's family has rented was built long ago by a bloodthirsty pirate! Sam convinces Jennie that where there's a pirate, there must be buried treasure ... and a ghost. What else could explain the creepy housekeeper, the threatening notes and the eerie sounds coming from the attic?

Strange Neighbors

There's a mystery brewing right next door to Sam! Three very odd women have moved in, bringing with them all sorts of caged animals. Sam is sure her creepy new neighbors are witches. After all, those poor animals look so miserable they must be under a spell. Suddenly Sam isn't feeling well either. Have the witches put a hex on her, too?

Aliens in Woodford

There are strange goings-on at Woodford's abandoned airfield — unexplained lights, transport trucks rumbling about in the middle of the night and security guards who seem to have superhuman strength. For Sam, it can mean only one thing — an alien invasion is on the way. In fact, the aliens may have already beamed up a couple of neighborhood pets!

A Weekend at the Grand Hotel

What could be more exciting than the bustling lobby of the Grand Hotel? Guests arrive, people meet — and signals are exchanged. For Sam, this can mean only one thing: spies, and lots of them! Why else would people be passing envelopes back and forth, sneaking into guests' rooms and using the back stairs instead of the elevator?

The Secret of Sagawa Lake

A whole weekend away at an island cabin in the woods. Could anything be more boring? Sam knows she'll never find a good mystery in a bunch of trees. But when the sheepdog sleuth and Jennie and Beth discover an old diary, the age-worn pages reveal some surprising secrets. Now Sam is sure there's a monster in the lake, and she's determined to track down its watery lair.

The Mummy Lives!

Sam can't find a mystery anywhere. The sheepdog sleuth doesn't know how she's going to make it through another winter. But things begin to heat up when Jennie and Beth visit a museum. There they see the mummy of a pharaoh who is said to walk the earth searching for his beloved missing dog!

Now Sam has the mummy hot on her trail. Will she be able to elude this creepy corpse as he stalks Woodford looking for his shaggy white dog?

Mary Labatt

Mary Labatt enjoys a special connection with children, having been involved in elementary education for over 25 years. Formerly the editor of an award-winning teachers' magazine, Labatt also taught elementary school.

Kids love listening to Labatt when she visits classrooms to talk about her books and her relationship with the real-life Sam. "Sam was a real character," she laughs. "Like her fictional counterpart, Sam really believed she was human, preferring the couch to the floor and pizza to dog food, which she refused to touch." Labatt still misses her sheepdog friend, even though Sam died 15 years ago. "Every now and then a creature comes along with whom you have a special connection. If you're lucky, you'll have known a Sam."

Labatt now writes fiction full-time and has several projects in the works. Sharing her busy life are her husband and their three children. "Today my house is filled with papers, children, hamsters, guinea pigs and, of course, a dog," she laughs. Labatt lives in Port Rowan, Ontario.